GRUSHA

BARBARA BUSTETTER FALK

A Laura Geringer Book

An Imprint of HarperCollins*Publishers*

Grusha
Copyright © 1993 by Barbara Bustetter Falk
Printed in the U.S.A. All rights reserved.

Library of Congress Cataloging-in-Publication Data
Falk, Barbara Bustetter.
 Grusha / by Barbara Bustetter Falk.
  p.   cm.
 "A Laura Geringer book."
 Summary: After being captured for a Russian circus, Grusha the bear
learns his tricks well, but despite his new-found fame, he longs to return
to the forest.
 ISBN 0-06-021299-3. — ISBN 0-06-021300-0 (lib. bdg.)
 1. Bears—Juvenile fiction. [1. Bears—Fiction.   2. Circus—Fiction.
3. Soviet Union—Fiction.]   I. Title.
PZ10.3.F17Gr 1993   92-14980
[E]—dc20   CIP
                                                          AC

Typography by Christine Kettner
1 2 3 4 5 6 7 8 9 10 ❖
First Edition

For Marilyn

B.B.F.

GRUSHA lived in a forest so thick and damp, the trees dripped. In bogs of black mud, he knew how to find the tastiest bugs and the juiciest roots. He knew how to search through marsh grasses for bulbs, how to climb the tallest trees, and how to wade into a mountain stream and grab salmon as they swam by.

Grusha's favorite meal was honey. When he found a hive, he would slap at the bees one by one, stirring up the nest until the very last of the swarm was out. Then his long tongue would work back and forth, back and forth, licking up the sweet gold.

One spring morning, his nose was so full of the good scent of honey that he missed the smell of strangers in the woods. Suddenly a heavy net dropped from the trees, trapping Grusha where he stood.

Too surprised to protest, he found himself in a dark cage. He clicked his claws against the bars and whined, making a strange noise that sounded like a cross between a tap dance and the deep drone of a mosquito. Swaying back and forth with his eyes closed, he tried to picture his home in the wilderness. But he was too sad and frightened. At last, exhausted, he fell asleep.

The next morning, a smiling man unlocked the door to Grusha's cage. He held a chain that he linked to Grusha's collar, speaking gently to him as he stroked the bear's furry ears.

"My name is Peter," he said.

Peter was a circus trainer. He lived all alone in a small hut on the outskirts of the village. It was said that birds and foxes came to his call, that eels ate cheese out of his hand, and that his house was open to any animal that passed by.

"I'll teach you how to stand on your hind legs, my friend," he told Grusha. "How to bow and shake hands. How to jump and catch a ball. How to dance the lezginka. But best of all, I'll teach you how to ride a bicycle."

Grusha shook his head and groaned. He didn't want to learn all those things. He just wanted to go home.

Peter visited Grusha every day, and every day he had a treat for the bear. Sometimes it was fruit and nuts. Sometimes it was honey.

One day Peter said, "It's time to start, my friend."

He led Grusha over to a big tent. In the center of the tent was a tall pole, as tall as the tallest tree in Grusha's forest home. And leaning against the pole was something Grusha had never seen before. It was a bicycle.

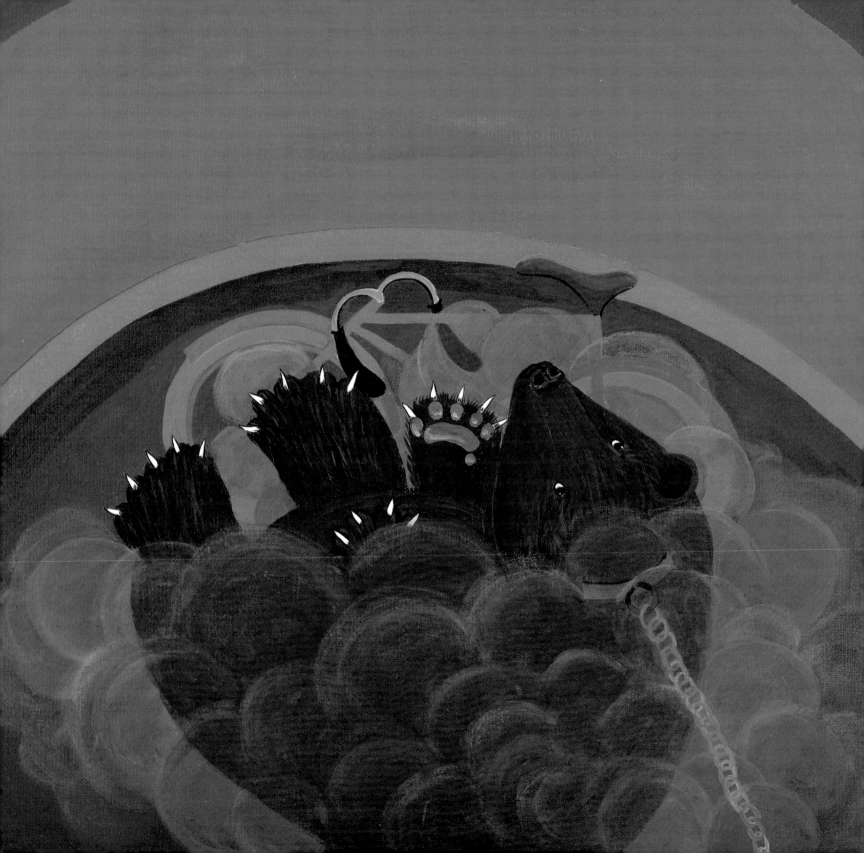

Grusha liked Peter and wanted to please him. But riding a bicycle was not easy. Grusha got up on the seat as Peter directed. But the bicycle crashed to the ground in a great cloud of dust. Grusha got up on the seat again. Crash. On the third try, Grusha stayed up long enough to make the pedals go around. Away he rolled.

Peter gave Grusha a treat of chestnuts and white bread. He brushed his coat clean and patted him on the back.

"We must practice every day, Grusha," he said.

When the weather got cold, Grusha wanted to sleep, so Peter had to keep him from napping. He rose two or three times during the night to take Grusha for brisk trots around the grounds, encouraging him all the while. "You're going to be a star," Peter said. "If you think you're going to find a hole and snooze until spring, you're not the bear I take you for."

Grusha put his paw on his trainer's head and licked his face. Then he blinked, yawned, sneezed, stretched, and got ready to practice. First one paw off the handlebars! Then two paws! Finally, Grusha could stand on his head on the seat while riding at high speed. He could even ride backward! He felt as if he were flying through the air. For the first time since he was captured, he forgot about the forests and bogs, the marshes and meadows of home. He felt free.

Soon Grusha was doing his act in the center ring. The crowds applauded. Little children waved banners that spelled "Grusha." Peter was right. Grusha had become a star.

Grusha inspired the other performers to new heights. The circus dogs jumped through higher hoops and learned how to play soccer. Wearing team jerseys, they ran back and forth, nudging the ball with their noses. The elephants dressed up as nurses and pushed giant carriages carrying baby elephants around the ring. The trapeze artists did double loops without a net. And Grusha himself perfected a new stunt—the triple forward roll.

Grusha became the toast of the town. And the toast of the circus as well. Everyone loved the bear who could ride a bicycle.

Then winter set in and the skies grew stormy. As the weather got colder and colder, Grusha longed to curl up in a nice warm cave and hibernate. He didn't want to be a star anymore. He wanted to go back to being just a bear.

One morning, after a thunderstorm, Peter tried to wake him for breakfast but Grusha wouldn't stir. He tried tempting the bear with honey, but Grusha just sniffed, growled, and rolled over.

He was having a nightmare.

The next day, Grusha's performance did not go well.
His bike wobbled and his somersaults were slow. His friends
began making mistakes too. The fire eater burned his
tongue. The trapeze artists couldn't find their trapezes. No
one turned on the spotlight. When the bareback rider tried
to put her head in the lion's mouth, the lion merely yawned.
And the dog who sang the Russian National Anthem gave
up and simply howled.

Peter watched it all sadly and shook his head.

Soon, Grusha had another dream. He dreamed he was riding his bicycle, but not in the ring. He dreamed he was riding his bicycle through a forest so thick that the trees dripped, through bogs of black mud, through banks of marsh grasses, through spring meadows, through mountain streams. He dreamed he was riding home.

When he woke up, it was dawn. Peter was sitting next to him, watching him with the same sad look. For a long moment, the man and the bear just gazed at one another. Then Peter gave Grusha a hug. "Good-bye," said his friend softly. "I'll miss you." And with that, he left.

Grusha blinked. Had Peter been part of his dream? Then he saw it, leaning against the corner of his cage. His bicycle. And beside it, on the ground, the lock to his door. He was free!

Grusha jumped on his bicycle and rode with all his might, faster than ever before. He rode without looking back. The rising sun caught the gleam of his whirring wheels as he pedaled along. After a while, he began to see things he remembered.

The moon rose, lighting silver ripples in an icy stream. Grusha stopped for a swim. A wolf howled, and then another. A moose trumpeted for his mate. The wind in the trees sounded sweet, like distant applause.

Grusha sighed a long and happy sigh. He was home at last.